RED eyes
AT NiGHT

MICHAEL MORPURGO
RED eyes AT NiGHT

Illustrated by Tony Ross

Hodder
Children's
Books

A division of Hachette Children's Books

CONTeNTS

For
Ted and Dorothy
and
their grandchildren

CHAPTER ONE

LiTTLe TOAD

My cousin Geraldine is a real little
toad. Every summer holidays it's the
same – Geraldine comes to stay.

And who has to look after her? I do,
because there's no-one else.

Dad's away all week. He always is.
He's in saucepans. "I'm in saucepans."
He's always saying that. It means he
sells them – his little joke.

Mum goes to work before
breakfast every morning – nursing.
And that's another thing. It's no fun
having a nurse for a mum.

She always knows when I'm pretending – pretending to be ill when I'm not, when I don't want to go to school.

That leaves just Gran and me, and Gran's got bad knees and can't get about much. So *I* get lumbered with Geraldine.

I have a good old moan about it, just like I am now, but no-one listens.

"She'll be company for you, Millie," says Mum. "Just look after her, there's a dear. And be nice."

Be nice! To Geraldine?!

Geraldine is only eight, two years younger than me, but you wouldn't know it. "Mature", Mum calls her. A stuck-up, hoity-toity little toad, that's what I call her.

She's so perfectly perfect – always eats everything on her plate, does her teeth twice a day, makes her bed, does her hair,  and she says her pleases and thank yous so often and so sweetly it makes you sick.

Worse, much worse, she's so *good* at things, everything. She plays her cello so well you actually want to listen.

She can do ten cartwheels one after the other, stand on her head for five minutes at a time, and she can tap-dance just like they do in *Riverdance*.

I could put up with all that – just about – but when Geraldine comes to stay she sleeps in *my* bedroom, in *my* bed. (I have to go on a mattress on the floor.) She plays with *my* computer and reads *my* books – she never asks!

And of course she's got a *bigger* room than mine at home, she says, a *miles* more up-to-date computer, she says, and a *million* more books.

But what really gets up my nose is Bingo. Bingo is my dog. I rescued him from  the RSPCA. He's a lurcher-cross-whippet and my most adorable thing in the entire world. He's got eyes that melt your heart.

Normally, normally, Bingo loves me to bits, and only me, but not when Geraldine's around.

I don't know what it is about her, but he follows her everywhere. He sleeps with her on my bed. He even comes when she calls him. He brings balls back when she throws them for him. He never does that for me.

There are times I could cheerfully send Bingo back where he came from – and Geraldine could go with him too.

CHAPTER TWO

THE REAL JIMJAMS

So this summer, as usual, Geraldine turns up, parks her cello in the hallway, and makes herself at home right away. Bingo's all over her, and Gran's cooing on and on about how much she's grown up, how pretty she looks, and what a proper young lady she is.

Proper pain in the neck, if you ask me.

Anyway, there we are, the two of us, lying there in bed that first night, the rain lashing against the window, the thunder rumbling around the house. Suddenly Bingo starts whimpering in the darkness.

"What's the matter with him?" asks Geraldine.

"It's the thunder," I tell her. "He's frightened of the thunder. Always has been."

"Well I'm not frightened of the thunder," she says.

White lightning fills the room, and then we're plunged back into pitch darkness as the thunder crashes right overhead. Bingo's whimpering from under the bed now.

"Millie?" says Geraldine, and she's sounding a little nervous.

"What?"

"I'm not frightened of the dark either, are you?"

"Course not."

Not true of course, but she's not to know that, is she?

"Nor me," she says. "And anyway, where I live in the country, it's darker than it is here, much darker. And even then I'm not frightened, not ever. Nothing to be frightened of, is there?"

"Just the ghost," I tell her. I don't know why I said it. It just popped out. I didn't mean anything, not to begin with.

There's this long silence.

Then she tries to laugh it off. But it's not a real laugh at all. I can tell. She's scared! Geraldine's scared!

And then, out of nowhere, I have this great idea. I'd seen it myself, when I was little, in Dad's garden shack. Gave me the real jimjams, and if it gave me the jimjams, then maybe . . .

"No such things as ghosts," she says. "Are there?"

"Course there are," I whisper. "We've got one of our own. He's got red eyes that glow in the dark."

21

"Red eyes," she breathes. Now I've really got her going.

"Honest," I tell her. "He lives in Dad's garden shack – well, most of the time anyway. He goes out at night, y'know, like ghosts do, for a walk around."

"He never!"

"I've seen him. I've seen him coming across the patio in the middle of the night, when everyone's gone to bed. And some nights, some nights, he even comes inside the house. He comes creeping, creeping up the stairs, along the landing. He turns taps on.

Leaves lights on. Switched on the telly
once. True. And, and, he smells. He
smells of pepper. I've smelt him. And
wherever he goes, it's all cold and
damp and shivery. I've felt him."

I'm doing well now, really well.
The silence from her bed tells me so.

When she does speak, there's a
wobble in her voice. "You're a liar,
Millie," she says. "You're a horrible
liar."

"I am not," I tell her.

Then the light goes on.

She's propped up on her elbows
and white as the sheets.

"All right, prove it then," she says.

"Go on, prove it."

"If you like." I'm thinking now, thinking hard. I need time, time to work things out, to arrange things, if you know what I mean.

"Not tonight," I tell her, "it's no good tonight. He never comes out if it's like this. Maybe he hates rain. Or maybe he doesn't like thunder, like Bingo. But tomorrow night should be OK, if the rain stops that it." I turn over so she can't see me smiling.

"Better turn off the light," I go on. "Don't want to waste electricity. Unless you're frightened, of course."

"Course I'm not. And anyway, I don't believe you. So there. And you can't prove it, I know you can't."

"Nighty night," I'm trilling now. "Nighty night. Don't let the vampires bite."

"Don't be so silly. It's not funny, you know."

"Oh no, it's not funny," I tell her. "It's not funny at all," and I'm smothering my giggles the best I can.

After a while I hear her lie down, but she doesn't turn out the light.

The thunder storm is moving away. There are ten seconds between the lightning and the thunder now, so it's ten miles away. She still hasn't turned out the light.

I'm lying there trying to work out how I'm going to fix up "the red-eyed ghost" for her.

It wasn't going to be easy. I could do the pepper – that bit would be simple enough, but as for the rest . . .

Then I'm drifting off to sleep.

I can't help myself.

When I wake up the next morning the light's still on, and Geraldine's fast asleep with her thumb in her mouth, and Bingo's stretched out beside her, his nose in her ear.

I still haven't worked it all out, about "the red-eyed ghost". But you've got to have luck in this life, haven't you? The thing about luck is that you never know where it's coming from, nor when it's coming, either.

CHAPTER THREE

A LOT OF OLD CODSWALLOP

So there we are at breakfast, just Gran and Geraldine and Bingo and me. Gran's going on about lightning and how you mustn't stand under trees in a thunder storm, nor use the phone.

"I got struck once," she says. "While I was on the phone. Threw me clean across the room, it did. Dreadful it was, dreadful. I had a ringing in my head for a week."

Then I notice Geraldine, and so does Gran. She's not eating her cornflakes. She hasn't touched her toast either. She's just sitting there, looking all sad and thoughtful and sorry for herself.

Bingo knows it too. He's got his head on her lap, his eyes looking up at her all lovey-dovey and adoring. Mangey mutt!

"Anything the matter, dear?" Gran asks her, as she pours the tea. "You don't look yourself. Didn't you sleep well? Thunder kept you awake, did it?"

"Gran?" Geraldine's up to something. I can hear it in her voice. "Gran? Do you believe in ghosts?" She's going to drop me right in it. Little toad.

Gran's laughing away. "Ghosts? Of course not. Of course I don't. Codswallop, lot of old codswallop, that's what ghosts are. I believe in what I can see, nothing else. No such things as ghosts, except in stories, of course."

Geraldine's smiling at me across the table, her sickening told-you-so kind of smile.

"But Gran," she says, and she's still looking at me, still smiling, "just supposing there were ghosts – which there's not of course – but just supposing, they wouldn't have red eyes, would they? And they wouldn't smell of pepper, would they?"

"Red eyes? Pepper?" says Gran. "What is the matter with you this morning, Geraldine? What is all this? Ghosts that smell of pepper! Red eyes! Codswallop! Codswallop! No more of this nonsense, there's a good girl. Just eat your cornflakes, dear."

Before you can say "Kellogg's"

Geraldine has scoffed down her cornflakes *and* three pieces of toast, *and* she's feeding Bingo the crusts.

(Gran sees her doing it and she never says a thing!) I always have to eat my crusts, and I'm never allowed to feed Bingo from the table, either.

Worse, whenever Gran's not looking – Geraldine's thumbing her nose at me, sticking her thumbs in her ears and wriggling her fingers at me, or she's putting her tongue out at me. And do you know what she gets? I'll tell you.

She gets a "good girl" from Gran
for eating her cornflakes, *and* a kiss on
the head when she offers to help wash
up the breakfast.

So that's how I come to find
myself doing the
drying up, with Gran
pottering in and out
and Bingo hoovering
under the breakfast
table.

And every time Gran potters out
Geraldine flicks soapsuds in my face
or sticks her tongue out at me.
There's nothing I can do about it,
not with Gran pottering in again.

For the moment I just have to grin
and bear it. But not for long,
not for long.

CHAPTER FOUR

CAT ON A HOT TIN ROOF

After breakfast, we're outside playing in the garden. Geraldine does amazing things on climbing frames. She's hanging up by her toes, like a bat with knickers – if you know what I mean – when Bingo sees the next door's cat.

That cat's always taking liberties, sunning himself on the tin roof of

Dad's shack, and Bingo does not like it, not one bit, he never has. Suddenly he's streaking across the grass, hackles up and barking like crazy.

The cat's vanished already, but Bingo likes to make quite sure he doesn't come back. So he's standing by Dad's shack telling the cat just what he thinks of him.

"What's the matter with Bingo?" says upside-down Geraldine.

"It's the shack, Dad's garden shack. He doesn't like it, not since *he* moved in. They can sense things, dogs can."

"Yeah, yeah," she says, all sarcastic.

But then she swings herself upright and I notice she keeps glancing at Dad's shack, and at Bingo barking himself silly. And I know she's thinking about it. I know she's worried.

Later on the same morning we're down at the bottom of the garden climbing the crab-apple tree. And of course Geraldine has to climb faster and higher than me. She's sitting up there on the branch above, swinging her legs and laughing at me out of the sun.

"Do you know, Millie, that you get spots on your tongue if you lie?"

She's crowing at me now. "I bet you've got millions on your tongue. And anyway, I never believed you. All about the red eyes and the pepper and that. I never believed you. Ghosts are stupid. He's not real anyway, so there."

I put my finger to my lips and point at Dad's shack. "Sssh," I whisper. "You shouldn't. You mustn't."

"What d'you mean?"

"You mustn't talk about him. In case he's listening. He hates it when you talk about him. Makes him really angry. And when he's angry, the things he does. It makes me shiver just to think about it."

"Oh yeah." But then after a moment or two, she says: "What sort of things?"

"Y'know, ghostly sorts of things, *ghastly* sorts of things."

She's snorting at me now, pretending she doesn't believe any of it. But I know better. So I go on. "He rattles doors. He howls around the house. He leaves pools of blood on the kitchen floor.

And if he's really mad, he comes up behind you and puts his clammy hands around your throat. Then he . . ."

"Stop," she's screaming at me now. "I don't want to hear it. I don't want to hear it." I look up. She's got her hands over her ears. "I don't believe it. I don't believe any of it."

"All right," I tell her, shrugging my shoulders. "You asked. I was just telling you, that's all. You believe what you like. See if I care."

"It's not true, it can't be. Gran said there's no such thing as ghosts. She said it was all codswallop. So."

And then it comes to me, just like that, out of the blue. Call it intuition, call it inspiration, call it genius. Call it what you like. I'd worked it all out, the whole thing, in an instant.

"It's that word," I tell her, hushing my voice so I sound very mysterious.

"What word?"

"Codswallop. It's a sort of secret code, so we don't upset him. If anyone talks about him, if anyone even just says the word 'ghost,' one of us has to say 'codswallop'. Dad fixed it up with him years ago. It means sorry. But you can't go around saying 'sorry' to no-one, can you? People'd think we're all mad, bonkers. So we say 'codswallop' instead. He hears us and he doesn't get angry. Simple. Didn't you notice how Gran kept saying it when you were asking about ghosts at breakfast? Codswallop. Codswallop. She kept saying it. Don't you remember?"

Suddenly Geraldine's legs aren't swinging any more. "But she said. Gran said. She said she didn't believe in . . . them. She told me they weren't true."

"Course she did. She didn't want to frighten you, that's all. But then, you're not frightened of anything much, are you? Not even ghosts."

I clap my hand over my mouth. "Codswallop," I say, all muffled under my hand. "Codswallop. Codswallop. Codswallop."

Geraldine sits there for a moment or two in silence. I can *hear* her thinking, I really can. Bingo's stopped his barking at last and he's giving himself a good ear scratch instead.

Then, quick as you like, she's down the tree and on the ground, looking very nervously at Dad's garden shack. "I'm feeling sick," she says.

And off she goes running across the garden and around the goldfish pond towards the house, keeping herself well away from Dad's garden shack, I notice.

I almost feel sorry for her, but only almost.

CHAPTER FIVE

eNOUGH TO MAKe yOU SNeeZe

That evening we're all in the sitting-
room for Geraldine's cello concert,
Mum, Gran and me. Dad's still away,
of course. When I say "concert", I
really mean "practice". It's just
Geraldine doing her practice and for
some reason I'm not quite sure of,
we all have to sit there and listen,
and clap too.

Normally, like I've said – and I don't like to say it – but normally, Geraldine's brilliant on her cello.

It makes me sick she's so brilliant. But not this evening. This evening, I'm glad to say, Geraldine's cello playing is definitely not what it should be.

In fact it's dreadful. Every note
sets your teeth on edge. It's Prokofiev,
she says, and I can quite believe it.
It's like screeching chalk on a
blackboard.

Mum and Gran are giving each other worried looks, and Bingo has just slunk out of the room with his tail between his legs. Time for me to go too.

I creep out, and as I go I get a daggers look from Mum. "Toilet," I mouth at her, but I know she doesn't believe me.

Bingo comes out into the garden with me. Glad to get out, and I don't blame him. It's cold out there and I haven't much time, so I run. Bingo disappears into the dark of the garden, to do his business, I expect.

Now the thing is that no-one, *no-one*, is ever allowed in Dad's shack, unless he's there and unless he invites you. Gran calls it his "wendy house". It's his private hideyhole, where he keeps his "toy" – that's what Mum calls it anyway. They both tease him about it, but Dad takes no notice. He loves it in there. He spends hours fiddling about with it all.

He's taken me in once or twice, but a long time ago when I was little. To be honest I found it all a bit boring, but I do know how to switch it on. Well, I think I do. I hope I do. And for what I've got in mind, that's all I'll need.

I fumble around in the dark by the door of Dad's shack for the conch shell where he hides the key.

I let myself in. It's all musty in there, I can't see a thing. I can't risk turning on the light, so I have to find it in the dark, and that's not easy. Anyway, after a bit of groping about I find what I'm looking for and I switch it on. I'm in and out of the shed in under a minute.

All I need now is a little luck, the most important ingredient of all – and pepper, of course.

I creep back into the house and tiptoe to the kitchen. The pepper pot's just where it always is, on the rack by the cooker, the brown dusty kind – it's better for sneezing.

I pocket it swiftly and then I'm back
to the sitting room and back to
Geraldine's cello concert – which
is still excruciating.

Geraldine's looking really
miserable. It's like she's fighting her
cello, not playing it.

I get a "where-have-you-been"

look from Mum. I smile back at her
sweetly, and at Geraldine too. After
all, I tell myself, I've got a lot to smile
about.

If all goes to plan, and it should,
then tonight's going to be special, very
special indeed.

CHAPTER SIX

MY GRAND PLAN

Up and down, Geraldine is, like a
yo-yo. One minute down in the
dumps, the next she's happy as a lark.

I've done all the nighty-night hugs
with Gran and Mum and I'm upstairs
brushing my teeth when Geraldine
comes breezing into the bathroom,
all sparkly-eyed and happy. I can't
work out why. I don't have to ask.
She soon tells me.

"I asked your mum," she says,
squeezing out her toothpaste. I try not
to look worried, but I am. She's
grinning away as she brushes her
teeth.

"So? What'd you ask her then?" I
say.

"What d'you think? About your
silly red-eyed ghost that smells of
pepper, that's what."

She spits into the basin.

"That's what I think of you and your stupid lies. Your mum just said what Gran said. You know what she told me? She said you were making the whole thing up, that I wasn't to take any notice. I asked her all about 'codswallop'. Codswallop's not a secret code at all, is it?"

She gurgles noisily and then spits out again. "So you're just a liar, aren't you? Just a rotten liar." And she starts chanting at me. "Liar, liar, pants on fire. Nose is as long as a telephone wire.

Liar, liar . . ." And now she's not just chanting, she's tap-dancing around the bathroom. Tap-dancing little toad.

All right, I'm thinking, maybe
this is a setback, but it's not a
disaster. Just take it easy, play it
cool. "Mum *would* say that,
wouldn't she?" I tell her. "She doesn't
want you worrying, that's all. You

 think what you
like. You asked
for proof,
right?"
"Yes."

"Well, you're going to get it; and
when you do, then you'll have to
believe me, won't you? Could be
tonight, you never know."

Suddenly Geraldine's not dancing

any more. I've got her worried again.

"You've got toothpaste on your chin," I say, and I leave her standing there in the bathroom, her toothpastey mouth wide open and gaping after me.

* * *

It's later that night. I'm lying in the dark of the bedroom, just waiting, waiting for Mum and Gran and Geraldine to go off to sleep. It's been a long wait, but at last I hear Mum's radio go off. Gran's already snoring next door, and across the room Geraldine's breathing deeply and regularly – she has been for a long while.

It's time. I get up. Not a sound. I tiptoe out of the room, the pepper pot in my hand. Quiet as I can, I steal about the house sprinkling it everywhere – all over the corridor, down the stairs, in the hallway, till there's no more pepper left.

I go back upstairs, trying hard not
to sneeze, slip into my bedroom and
shake Geraldine awake.

"I can smell him," I'm whispering
and sniffing the air. "Peppery. Can
you smell it? And it's cold and damp
too. He's been here, right in this room.
I can feel it."

She's sniffing too, and then she's sitting bolt upright in bed. She's scared stiff.

"Pepper," she breathes. "It's pepper."

"Told you so, didn't I? Come on," I tell her. "I'll show you. He's probably back in Dad's shack by now."

I put on my dressing gown and slippers, but Geraldine's still just sitting there. I can see the whites of her eyes in the dark. "What's the matter?" I ask her.

"Nothing," she says.  "Not scared, are you?"

"Course not."

"It's all right," I tell her, ever so

nicely, ever so kindly. "He's quite safe. He never hurt anyone, not so far anyway."

She thinks about it for a few moments. "I know it's just a trick," she says. "It must be. He's not real, he can't be. Your mum said. Gran said."

"Only one way to find out," I tell her. "Are you coming or not?"

She's a while putting on her dressing-gown, but at last the two of us are creeping down the stairs.

The wind is rattling the bathroom window and whining down the chimney. The floorboards are creaking under our feet.

It's perfect. The kitchen door even groans on its hinges as I open it. It's all just as it should be, just like a real horror film.

For some reason Geraldine doesn't seem to want to come any further. I take her gently by the hand, and I feel her holding on tight, very tight.

"It's all right," I tell her, ever so nicely, ever so kindly. "It's all right."

Across the garden I can see the dark looming shape of Dad's garden shack.

"He's in there?" whispered Geraldine. "He's really in there?"

"Probably," I say. "Come on."

And so, still clutching my hand, she comes with me, tiptoeing across the lawn, her grip tightening with every step.

Then, bent double, we're running. Breathless, we reach Dad's shack and crouch down under the window ledge.

I close my eyes and hope hard. Then, squeezing her hand, we both stand up slowly, inch by inch, and peep in at the window.

For several moments there's nothing but darkness in there, just blackness; and I'm thinking something must have gone wrong.

Then suddenly it happens, exactly as I'd hoped. Two red eyes are glowing at us from the back of the shed.

On.

Off.

On.

Off.

And then, somewhere close by, an owl hoots, the echoes of it filling the night sky. Brilliant, just brilliant. I couldn't have arranged it better.

Too woo
Too Woo Woo Woo
Too Woo

Geraldine's hand is suddenly not gripping any more. I look around, and there she is, stretched out on the grass at my feet. She's fainted clean away.

And I'm thinking: she can't do that. She's not supposed to do that. That's not part of my grand plan at all.

CHAPTER SEVEN

RUBBeR DUCK

Now I'm really panicking. What am I going to do? I can't call for help, can I? Not after what I've done.

I look around me and I see the goldfish pond. That gives me an idea.

I scoop up handfuls of water, carry it back and splosh it all over Geraldine's face until at last she opens her eyes.

At that same moment, we hear this strange unearthly voice, and it's coming from the inside of the shed.

"Come in. Come in. Is anyone out there? Come in.
Come in."

Then there's something scratching at the door, trying to claw its way out, and it's shrieking and howling. The blood goes cold in my veins.

Geraldine screams.

I scream.

We're both clutching each other and screaming blue murder, but the scratching goes on and the howling and that dreadful voice telling us to come in.

"I know you're out there. Come on. I know you're out there."

And then the owl's hooting again.

TooWoo TooWoo Woo Woo TooWoo

Still the ghost keeps calling us and howling piteously and still he claws at the door, and the door's shaking and rattling in its frame. I want to get up and run but I can't. I can't move.

I'm frozen where I am. All I can do is scream like Geraldine, only louder, louder, so I don't have to hear the ghost's deathly voice, and his blood-curdling shrieks.

* * *

Suddenly the lights in the house go on, then every light in the street. Then Mum and Gran are running towards us across the garden, dressing gowns flying.

"The red-eyed ghost!" Geraldine sobs. "He's in there, in the shack. I've seen him. I've *heard* him."

They look at us as if we're mad.

"It's true," I tell them. "The ghost, he's coming to get us. He's clawing his way out." And I'm sobbing too. I can't stop myself.

 Then Gran's cuddling us close, while Mum walks over to Dad's shack and peers in through the window.

"Come in." The same voice again, but louder. "Come in. This is

Rubber Duck, Rubber Duck, calling Armadillo. Are you there, Armadillo? Are you there? Come in, please. This is Rubber Duck, Rubber Duck."

"That's no ghost," says Mum. "That's your Dad's CB radio, his toy. He's got friends that call him up from all over the world. Rubber Duck's one of them, I expect. Always give themselves funny names, they do."

Then more scratching at the door, more howling. Mum goes round and fishes for the key in the conch shell. She opens the door.

You've guessed it. Out comes
Bingo, yowling and barking and
whimpering all at once. I'd locked
him in by mistake.

Geraldine's
not sobbing any
more, and
neither am I.
I'm kicking
myself instead.
I should have
known. It

should have been obvious. Why
didn't I think of it? How could I have
been so stupid?

Mum's coming back towards us, towards me, Bingo gambolling around her. I'm for the high jump. I know it. Nothing I can do about it. No way out.

"Well, Millie," she says, and there are dark clouds scooting across the moon above her head, "you've been up to something, haven't you? All this red-eyed ghost nonsense, all this codswallop stuff. It's one of your little games, isn't it? Your dad would never leave his CB radio on. Never. No, someone's been in there and switched it on, haven't they? That's how Bingo got himself shut in there, isn't it?

Well, I didn't do it. Gran didn't do it.
Geraldine certainly didn't do it. And
nor did Bingo, I think. That leaves just
you."

There's no point in denying it.
Gran's not cuddling me any more.

She's still cuddling Geraldine though, and Geraldine's cuddling her back. There's a smile on her face like the cat that's got the cream. Little toad.

Mum helps me up. "I think we'd better talk, hadn't we, Millie?" she says. "Inside, in the kitchen."

Things are not looking good.

CHAPTER EIGHT

FUNNY OLD WORLD

Once inside Mum sits me down at the kitchen table where we have all our arguments and heart-to-heart chats. I don't like to look at her when she's angry. So I look down at my hands instead.

And so I tell her the whole thing – it's the only way – beginning to end,

how I don't like Geraldine coming to
stay, why I don't like Geraldine, my
grand plan, and how it had all gone
wrong.

She likes the bit where I scared
myself silly – I can tell – but it's the
only bit she does like. She's sighing at
me meaningfully.

"You haven't been very nice to

Geraldine, have you?" she says.

That "nice" word again.

"No."

"Tell you what," she says. "A deal.
I won't tell your dad about all this,
nor about your going into his shack,
but in return you've got to do
something for me."

"What?"

"You've got to be nice to
Geraldine. She's not that bad, and
anyway, she's your cousin. So from
now on, just be nice. And I mean very
nice. Well?"

"All right," I tell her. I haven't got much choice, have I?

"And you can start by saying sorry to her right now."

I go up the stairs very slowly indeed. I am not looking forward to this, not one bit. I open the bedroom door. It's dark in there. I take a deep breath, and then I just go in and say it. "I'm sorry Geraldine." She doesn't say anything. So I try again. "I said I'm sorry, Geraldine. I'm sorry if I frightened you."

That's when the wardrobe door opens and there's this white shape floating silently across the room. I'm screaming and I'm screaming.

The light goes on. Geraldine's standing there and she's pulling the sheet off her head. She's smiling at me. "Only me," she says, ever so sweetly.

"You're a toad, a real little toad."

"Takes one to know one," she says.
And then she's laughing and I'm
laughing, and Bingo's there bouncing
up and down barking his head off.

We've been best friends ever since
– all three of us. Funny old world,
isn't it?

About the author

Michael Morpurgo, OBE, was named the third Children's Laureate. He is the best-loved author of many books for children of all ages, including *Private Peaceful*, *Kensuke's Kingdom* and *Farm Boy*. His bestselling novel *War Horse* has been very successfully adapted as a film and a play. Michael lives in Devon, with his wife Clare, where they run the charity Farms for City Children.

About the illustrator

Tony Ross is one of today's most recognised and popular illustrators. His own picture book series about Kitty the Princess began with the bestselling *I Want My Potty*. He has illustrated all the books in Francesca Simon's Horrid Henry series, as well as the Dr Xargle books by Jeanne Willis. For Hodder Children's Books, he has illustrated Ian Whybrow's popular Books for Boys series. Tony lives in Oxfordshire.

WRITTEN BY IAN WHYBROW   ILLUSTRATED BY TONY ROSS

**FROM FOOTBALL TO GO KARTING, FROM REAL HEROES
TO ALIENS, BOOKS FOR BOYS ARE PACKED WITH ACTION,
ADVENTURE AND LAUGHS!**

www.hodderchildrens.co.uk